JE READER

A Note to Parents and Caregivers:

Read-it! Readers are for children who are just starting on the amazing road to reading. These beautiful books support both the acquisition of reading skills and the love of books.

 The PURPLE LEVEL presents basic topics and objects using high frequency words and simple language patterns.

 The RED LEVEL presents familiar topics using common words and repeating sentence patterns.

 The BLUE LEVEL presents new ideas using a larger vocabulary and varied sentence structure.

 The YELLOW LEVEL presents more challenging ideas, a broad vocabulary, and wide variety in sentence structure.

 The GREEN LEVEL presents more complex ideas, an extended vocabulary range, and expanded language structures.

 The ORANGE LEVEL presents a wide range of ideas and concepts using challenging vocabulary and complex language structures.

When sharing a book with your child, read in short stretches, pausing often to talk about the pictures. Have your child turn the pages and point to the pictures and familiar words. And be sure to reread favorite stories or parts of stories.

There is no right or wrong way to share books with children. Find time to read with your child, and pass on the legacy of literacy.

Adria F. Klein, Ph.D.
Professor Emeritus
California State University
San Bernardino, California

Editor: Jill Kalz
Designer: Joe Anderson
Creative Director: Keith Griffin
Editorial Director: Carol Jones
The illustrations in this book were created using mixed media.

Picture Window Books
5115 Excelsior Boulevard
Suite 232
Minneapolis, MN 55416
877-845-8392
www.picturewindowbooks.com

Printed in the United States of America.

Library of Congress Cataloging-in-Publication Data
Shaskan, Trisha Speed.
Another pet / by Trisha Speed Shaskan ; illustrated by Kenneth Vincent.
p. cm. — (Read-it! readers)
Summary: After a trip to the zoo, Dennis wants a pet in addition to his dog Snips,
but when he considers the challenges of housing a giraffe or an octopus, he has
second thoughts.
ISBN-13: 978-1-4048-2404-1 (hardcover)
ISBN-10: 1-4048-2404-9 (hardcover)
[1. Pets—Fiction. 2. Zoo animals—Fiction. 3. Terriers—Fiction. 4. Dogs—Fiction.
5. Asian Americans—Fiction.] I. Vincent, Kenneth, ill. II. Title. III. Series.
PZ7.S53242Ano 2006
[E]—dc22   2006003574

Another Pet

by Trisha Speed Shaskan
illustrated by Kenneth Vincent

Special thanks to our advisers for their expertise:

Adria F. Klein, Ph.D.
Professor Emeritus, California State University
San Bernardino, California

Susan Kesselring, M.A.
Literacy Educator
Rosemount–Apple Valley–Eagan (Minnesota) School District

My name is Dennis.

And this is my dog, Snips. Snips is a good pet.

Yesterday, I went to the zoo with Snips. When I saw all of the animals, I wanted another pet.

What if I had a monkey for a pet? If I had a
monkey, it would climb up the window and pull
down the curtains.

That would not be good.

What if I had an octopus for a pet? If I had an octopus, it would never leave the bathtub.

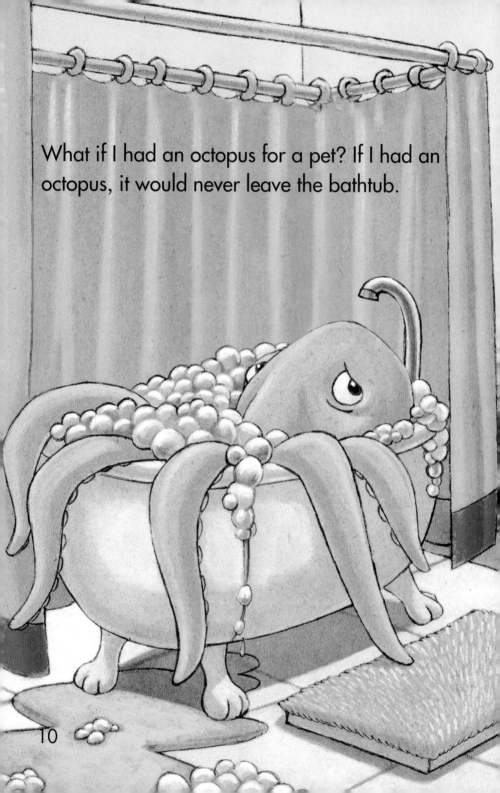

That would not be good.

What if I had a giraffe for a pet? If I had a giraffe, its head would poke a hole in the roof.

That would not be good.

What if I had an owl for a pet? If I had an owl, it would keep me awake all night.

*boot
boot*

That would not be good.

What if I had a penguin for a pet? If I had a penguin, it would eat everything in the freezer—even the ice cream!

That would not be good.

What if I had an elephant for a pet? If I had an
elephant, it would make a mess in the living room.

That would not be good.

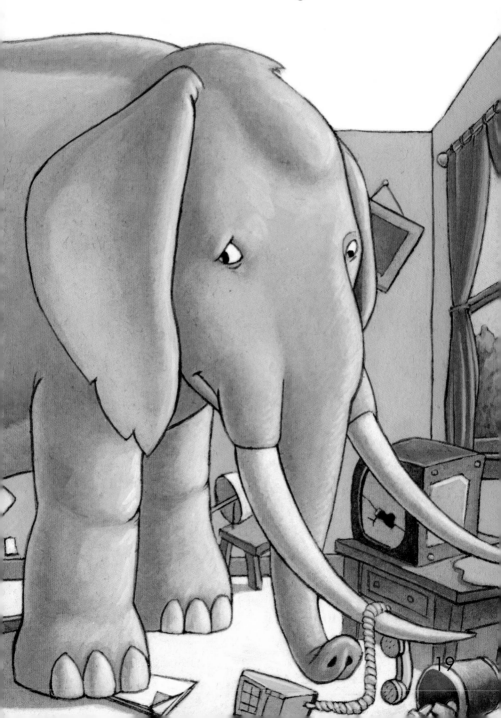

What if I had a seal for a pet? If I had a seal, it would bark louder than Snips.

That would not be good.

Maybe I don't need another pet after all.

Snips is the perfect pet for me!

More *Read-it!* Readers

Bright pictures and fun stories help you practice your reading skills. Look for more books at your level.

Alex and Sarah 1-4048-1352-7
Alex and the Team Jersey 1-4048-1024-2
Alex and Toolie 1-4048-1027-7
Felicio's Incredible Invention 1-4048-1030-7
Izzie's Idea 1-4048-0644-X
Joe's Day at Rumble's Cave Hotel 1-4048-1339-X
Naughty Nancy 1-4048-0558-3
Parents Do the Weirdest Things! 1-4048-1031-5
The Princess and the Frog 1-4048-0562-1
The Princess and the Tower 1-4048-1184-2
Rumble Meets Harry Hippo 1-4048-1338-1
Rumble Meets Lucas Lizard 1-4048-1334-9
Rumble Meets Randy Rabbit 1-4048-1337-3
Rumble Meets Shelby Spider 1-4048-1286-5
Rumble Meets Todd Toad 1-4048-1340-3
Rumble Meets Vikki Viper 1-4048-1342-X
Rumble's Famous Granny 1-4048-1336-5
Rumble the Dragon's Cave 1-4048-1353-5
The Three Princesses 1-4048-2422-7
The Truth About Hansel and Gretel 1-4048-0559-1
Willie the Whale 1-4048-0557-5

Looking for a specific title or level? A complete list of *Read-it!* Readers is available on our Web site:
www.picturewindowbooks.com